#1

The Secret of the Knight's Sword

by
**Carolyn Keene and
Franklin W. Dixon**

Illustrated by Paul Frame

WANDERER BOOKS
Published by Simon & Schuster, Inc., New York

Designed by Stanley S. Drate

Manufactured in the United States of America

10 9 8 7 6 5 4 3 2 1

NANCY DREW, NANCY DREW MYSTERY STORIES, and
THE HARDY BOYS are trademarks of Stratemeyer
Syndicate, registered in the United States
Patent and Trademark Office.
BE A DETECTIVE MYSTERY STORIES is a
trademark of Stratemeyer Syndicate.

WANDERER and colophon are registered trademarks
of Simon & Schuster, Inc.

Library of Congress Cataloging in Publication Data

Keene, Carolyn.
    The secret of the knight's sword.
    (Nancy Drew/the Hardy boys be a detective mystery stories #1)
    Summary: In England to discover the secret of the
Silver Knight in Bromley Hall, Carson Drew and his
daughter Nancy encounter Frank and Joe Hardy in their
hotel and the four proceed to unravel the mystery. The
reader's choices determine the direction of the
investigation.
    1. Plot-it-yourself stories. [1. Plot-it-yourself stories.
2. Mystery and detective stories] I. Dixon, Franklin W.
II. Title. III. Series: Keene, Carolyn. Nancy Drew/
the Hardy boys be a detective mystery stories #1.
PZ7.K23Se   1984   [Fic]   83-19682
ISBN 0-671-49919-X

Dear Fans,

Since so many of you have written to us saying how much you want to be detectives like Nancy Drew and The Hardy Boys, we figured out a way. Of course, we had to put our heads together to create mysteries that were so baffling they needed help from everyone including Nancy, Frank, Joe and you!

In these exciting new BE A DETECTIVE MYSTERY STORIES™ you'll be part of a great team of amateur sleuths following clues and wily suspects. At every turn you'll have a chance to pick a different trail filled with adventures that may lead to danger, surprise or an amazing discovery!

The choices are all yours—see how many there are and have fun!

C.K. and F.W.D.

"Watch out, Frank! That car's going too fast!" Joe Hardy pointed to a green Ford that was zooming toward them in the direction of London.

His older brother Frank, who was at the wheel of their rented sedan, swerved to the side of the road.

"Wow!" Joe sighed with relief as the speeding automobile whizzed safely past.

"I managed to read the license plate," announced their friend Nancy Drew. The titian-haired detective was in the back seat with her father, Carson Drew, a well-known lawyer. He snapped open his briefcase and jotted down the number Nancy gave him.

"Good work," he said. "We'll report that speeding Ford to the police when we arrive at Bromley Hall."

"Have you come to England to settle Lord Bromley's estate, Mr. Drew?" Frank asked.

"No, my reason for this visit is more unusual than that," the lawyer replied mysteriously.

Turn to page 2.

2

"You sound just like our dad," Joe said, turning his blond head to look at Mr. Drew. "He came to England on a top-secret mission and wouldn't tell us a word about it."

Fenton Hardy was a private investigator who often handled assignments in foreign countries. His sons, amateur detectives in their own right, had come along to London with him, where, to their surprise, they had found Nancy and her father staying at the same hotel near Hyde Park.

Mr. Drew smiled at Joe's remark. "The request that brought me here is not top secret. Shortly before Lord Bromley died last month, he sent me a strange message. Here, I'll read it to you."

The lawyer removed a parchment letter from his briefcase and read:

"The Silver Knight of Bromley Hall holds a secret. To find it, press the lion's eye on the knight's sword. Then twist the hilt to the right."

"That's all?" Frank asked.

"That's it," Mr. Drew replied.

Nancy took the piece of paper and held it against the light. "Look, there's a watermark. It appears to be a knight in a suit of armor. I hadn't noticed it before."

Turn to page 3.

3

"That must be the Silver Knight," Mr. Drew explained. "My father, an old friend of Lord Bromley's, told me that the Silver Knight was very important to the Bromley family. The suit of armor belonged to a famous ancestor of theirs and has been handed down from generation to generation."

"We'll soon see the knight for ourselves," Frank said, leaning his dark-haired head close to the windshield. "I believe Bromley Hall is just ahead."

As he turned into the estate's driveway, a black Rolls-Royce passed them, driving away from the house. Joe watched it until it was out of sight.

"Did you see that driver?" he asked. "He appeared to be really nervous. When he saw us, he nearly jumped out of his seat!"

"I noticed it, too," Nancy declared.

Frank stopped in front of Bromley Hall, a large house built of dark, gray stone. As everyone got out, a man hurried down the front steps.

"Mr. Drew, I presume," he said. "I'm Jenkins, the butler. I'm afraid something terrible has happened. Come this way, please."

Turn to page 4.

4

"What's the problem?" Mr. Drew asked as the visitors followed the butler inside.

"Something was stolen," the man replied as he led them into the large entrance hall.

Nancy stared in awe at the magnificent suit of armor mounted on a pedestal near the grand staircase.

"The Silver Knight!" she exclaimed.

"But where's his sword?" Joe asked, pointing to the knight's outstretched, empty right hand.

"Gone!" the butler uttered with dismay. "The Silver Knight's sword has been stolen!"

"And with it, Lord Bromley's secret," Mr. Drew added in a hushed voice.

Turn to page 5.

"Do you have any idea how it happened, or who could have taken it?" Frank asked Jenkins.

The butler shook his head in confusion. "No, I only noticed that the sword was missing a few minutes before you drove up."

5

"We should get to work right away while the thief's trail is still fresh!" Frank declared. "There may be some important clues around here."

"That green car that passed us on the road to London," Nancy said thoughtfully. "I wonder if the driver was making a fast escape from Bromley Hall."

"And what about the Rolls-Royce we passed in the driveway?" Joe added. "Do you remember how nervous that guy looked?"

If you think Nancy and the Hardy boys should stay at Bromley Hall and investigate, turn to page 6.
If you think they should follow the trail of the green car to London, turn to page 10.
If you think they should investigate the driver of the Rolls-Royce, turn to page 12.

6

Frank went out to their car to get his fingerprinting kit while Nancy and Joe began to examine the Silver Knight for clues.

Just then, a young woman wearing riding clothes entered the hallway.

"You must be Carson Drew," she said as she walked up to shake the lawyer's hand. "I'm Lord Bromley's granddaughter, Elizabeth."

Carson Drew introduced Nancy and Joe Hardy to Elizabeth. Then he quickly explained, "We've just learned some bad news. The knight's sword has been stolen."

Elizabeth's face turned pale and her eyes took on a look of fright. "The curse," she murmured. "An old legend says that a curse will fall on the Bromley family if anything happens to the Silver Knight."

"Don't worry, Elizabeth," Mr. Drew assured her. "We'll do our best to—"

He was interrupted by a shout from Joe Hardy.

"Look out, Elizabeth!" Then the blond detective lunged toward the young woman, pushing her away from where she stood.

Seconds later, a large, plaster object smashed against the floor in the exact spot where Elizabeth had stood.

Turn to page 8.

8

"The curse has come true!" Elizabeth shuddered.

Jenkins stooped down to examine the shattered pieces. "This was a statue that stood at the top of the stairs. It must have fallen down by accident."

"Or it was pushed," Nancy added, gazing up at the open staircase that wound above them.

As she uttered these words, a handsome young man, also wearing riding clothes, walked into the hallway.

"Philip!" Elizabeth cried out and ran to him. "The most awful things have happened," she sobbed.

"Who are these people, Elizabeth?" the young man asked in a cold voice as he glared at the visitors.

Elizabeth introduced the Americans and then added, "This is Philip Harrington, my fiancé." Suddenly, the young woman seemed overwhelmed by all that had happened. She began to tremble and swooned into her fiancé's arms.

"You must get some rest, Elizabeth," Philip ordered, leading her into the drawing room. He closed the door tightly behind them.

Turn to page 9.

Meanwhile, Frank had come back into the house. "That guy who came in just before me," he said. "Who is he?"

"Elizabeth Bromley's fiancé," Nancy answered. "Not a very friendly type."

"Well, I saw him running out of a thick hedge nearby," Frank said with suspicion. "He kept glancing back over his shoulder as if he was nervous about something. I think we should investigate what it was."

"There's something else we have to look into," Joe explained to his brother. "A statue just fell from the top of the staircase and almost hit Lord Bromley's granddaughter. Let's check the top floor of the house. It may have been pushed."

"While you're following up those clues, I'll report the speeder to the police," Mr. Drew added.

If you think Nancy and the Hardy boys should go outside to investigate the mysterious hedge, turn to page 15.

If you think they should check out the upstairs of Bromley Hall, turn to page 17.

10

"Where is a telephone?" Nancy asked Jenkins. "I'll call the police about that speeding car."

At that moment, a young woman walked into the hallway. Immediately, she sensed that something was wrong. "I'm Lord Bromley's granddaughter, Elizabeth," she explained. "Are you Carson Drew?"

"Yes, I am," Mr. Drew replied. "And this is my daughter, Nancy, and her friends Frank and Joe Hardy." Then he added solemnly, "We have some bad news, I'm afraid."

Elizabeth's eyes flitted around the room. "The knight's sword," she suddenly exclaimed. "What has happened to it?"

"It's been stolen, Miss Elizabeth," Jenkins replied.

The young woman's face turned pale. "The curse," she murmured in a frightened voice. "An old legend says a curse will fall on the Bromley family if anything happens to the Silver Knight."

"We're trying to find the thief who stole the sword," Nancy explained. "I have the license number of a green Ford that passed us, speeding on the road toward London."

"Green, did you say?" Elizabeth asked. "I saw an unfamiliar green car parked near the gate of the house only a half hour ago."

Turn to page 11.

"We can't waste any time," Frank said urgently. "Let's check that license number with the police."

While Nancy phoned the local authorities, Frank and Joe searched the place where Elizabeth had seen the green car. They returned to the house with a small slip of paper.

"Look," Joe said, handing the paper to Mr. Drew. "We found this in the grass near the gate."

"It's a rail ticket," Mr. Drew observed, "to Paddington Station. That's not far from our hotel in London."

Just then, Nancy returned from the telephone. "Our suspicions were correct about that green Ford," she announced. "The authorities traced the license plate to London. The police computers showed that the vehicle had just been reported as stolen."

"Let's head back to London right away," Frank suggested. "We can keep in touch with the police there."

"We'll inform you about any developments, Elizabeth," Mr. Drew said as they left the house.

"Don't worry," Joe assured her. "We'll find the sword and bring it back to Bromley Hall."

Turn to page 31.

12

"Who was that man in the Rolls-Royce, Jenkins?" Joe asked the butler.

Before Jenkins could answer, a young woman entered the hallway.

"You must be Carson Drew," she said as she walked up to shake the lawyer's hand. "I am Elizabeth Bromley, Lord Bromley's granddaughter."

Carson Drew introduced Nancy and the Hardy brothers to Elizabeth. Then he added, "We've just learned that the knight's sword has been stolen."

A look of shock came over Elizabeth's face. "Who would do a thing like that?" she asked in dismay.

"We think we have a clue," Nancy answered. "As we drove up to Bromley Hall, a suspicious-looking man was leaving in a Rolls-Royce."

"That was Simon Pethick, my grandfather's solicitor," Elizabeth explained. "He is a trusted friend of the family's."

"What was Mr. Pethick doing at Bromley Hall today?" Carson Drew asked.

"He was working in grandfather's library," Elizabeth answered. "I did mention to him that you were coming. . . ." Suddenly, the young woman's face clouded over. "He seemed very upset about that. A short time later, I heard his car drive away."

Turn to page 13.

"Could you tell us where he lives?" Frank asked Elizabeth. "We should question him immediately."

After learning Simon Pethick's address, the three young detectives left Bromley Hall to drive to Kent, where the solicitor had a country house. It didn't take them very long to make the trip.

"There it is," Joe said, pointing out the window to a large, rambling home. "Pethick Manor."

As Frank pulled up in front of the house, the sleuths looked for the solicitor's Rolls-Royce. It was nowhere to be seen.

"I hope we can find Mr. Pethick," Joe said as they got out of their blue sedan. "If he did in fact steal the sword, he may be desperate enough to disappear from sight."

A middle-aged woman dressed in a maid's uniform answered their knock on the door.

"Do you want to see Mr. Pethick?" she asked. "You are a few minutes too late, I'm afraid. I just packed his flying gear. He's taking his plane to France today."

Turn to page 14.

14

"Did he tell you why he was going to France?" Nancy asked the woman.

"No, he didn't say. But he was in a nervous flurry to get away from here."

"Where does he keep his plane?" Frank asked urgently.

"Why, at the Channel airfield, near the coast," the maid answered. "I suppose he'll take off right after his appointment with Mr. Bromley."

"Mr. Bromley?" Joe asked curiously.

"Evan Bromley, Lord Bromley's grandson," the woman explained. She paused and then added, "Evan is the black sheep of the family. He lives not far from here in a cottage at 48 Wiley Way."

"Thank you very much," Nancy told the maid. Then the sleuths walked away from the house to their car.

"Every minute counts if we're going to catch Simon Pethick," Frank said worriedly. "I wonder where we should look for him?"

If you think the detectives should go to Evan Bromley's cottage, turn to page 16.

If you think they should drive to the airfield, turn to page 22.

"There certainly was something suspicious about Philip Harrington's behavior," Nancy said. "Let's investigate that hedge."

The three young sleuths hurried outside, leaving Mr. Drew in the hallway. Frank led Nancy and Joe to a high, thick hedge with a narrow opening.

The younger Hardy brother walked in first. "It looks like a maze!" he exclaimed. Nancy and Frank quickly joined him on a narrow path lined on both sides by bushes higher than their heads.

"It *is* a maze," Nancy said. "Whoever stole the sword might have hidden it in here."

Frank and Nancy both made diagrams of the maze as they followed its twists and turns. Shortly, they came to a place where the path forked in two directions.

"Let's split up," Nancy suggested. "I'll go to the right, and you go to the left."

"Okay," Frank agreed. "We'll meet back here in half an hour."

If you want to follow Nancy, turn to page 18.
If you want to follow Frank and Joe, turn to page 20.

16

Frank stopped at the nearest gas station to ask for directions to 48 Wiley Way.

"The cottage is only ten minutes away," he told Joe and Nancy. "We had better check on Evan Bromley and find out what he knows."

As the sleuths came to the cottage, they saw Simon Pethick's Rolls-Royce outside.

"Stop a short way down the road, Frank," Nancy suggested. "We don't want to announce our arrival."

After parking the car, Nancy, Frank, and Joe quietly approached the cottage. The small house was in disrepair and looked totally neglected by its owner.

As they came closer, the young detectives heard a conversation through the open windows. They concealed themselves behind a bush and listened.

"Grandfather wasn't as clever as he thought, Simon," a young man's voice said. "Here is the new will, hidden inside the knight's sword. I suppose he forgot that, long ago, he showed me how to open the hilt."

Turn to page 39.

"That statue didn't fall by accident," Nancy said angrily. "Someone must be upstairs."

Frank and Joe followed her up the staircase that wound at angles around an open stairwell three floors above them. As Nancy reached the landing to the second floor, she leaned against the old railing. With a brittle crack, part of it broke off and fell to the hallway below. For a second, Nancy seemed doomed to follow it. She teetered on the edge until Frank grabbed her from behind and pulled her back to safety.

"Whoever put a curse on Bromley Hall did a good job," Joe said, looking at the girl's pale face.

The titian-blond detective started to climb the stairs again. "Let's find out who is behind this," she declared.

The three sleuths soon reached the top floor of the house. As Nancy swept her carefully trained eyes over the walls of the hallway, her gaze fell upon a loose piece of molding in the wood paneling.

Curious, she stooped down to touch it. The wood gave way, and a secret panel swung open.

Turn to page 24.

18

Nancy set off down the path to the right. She carefully studied the ground for clues. In the soft earth, she detected fresh footprints. From their shape, the young detective deduced that they had been made by riding boots.

"Frank, Joe," she called out.

There was no answer. Nancy realized that the maze must have already led the Hardy boys too far in the opposite direction.

Stepping cautiously, she continued down the path. As she rounded a sharp corner, she suddenly came face to face with a burly, bearded man!

"What are you doing, snooping around here?" he snarled at her.

"Who are you?" the young detective demanded calmly.

"You'll never find out," the man hissed and grabbed Nancy's arms. Before she could call out for help, he tied a gag around her mouth.

The girl struggled desperately with her assailant as he pulled her deeper into the maze. Ahead, she saw a small hut with a thatched roof. The man pushed her inside and bound her hands behind her back.

Turn to page 19.

"Nobody will find you here for quite a while!" he said in a sinister voice. Then he laughed and slammed the door shut on her.

19

A moment later, Nancy heard a latch fall into place.

If you think the Hardy boys should rescue Nancy, turn to page 23.

If you think Nancy can escape by herself, turn to page 25.

20

Frank and Joe set off down the path to the left.

"I'll keep an eye out for clues," Joe commented to his brother. "You keep track of where we're going."

"I sure will," Frank said and grinned. "We don't want to get lost in this place."

As the path wound deeper and deeper into the maze, he carefully drew in each turn they made.

"Hey, Frank!" Joe suddenly called out. "Stop a minute. I think I've found something."

Frank went up to his brother, who was pulling a small object from the hedge.

"What is it?" Frank asked curiously.

"A feather," Joe replied and twirled it between two fingers. "But I've never seen a bird with green feathers like this. I suspect it's a dyed feather from a hat."

"Elizabeth's fiancé wasn't wearing a hat," Frank said. "Maybe someone else is roaming around in this maze with us."

He suddenly stopped talking and looked at Joe. Both had heard the sound of footsteps coming along the path on the other side of the hedge!

Turn to page 21.

The boys crouched down and tried to peer through the dense foilage. Their efforts to see were in vain, but they could tell by the sound of the heavy, fast footsteps that it was a man in a hurry.

"Let's follow the sounds of his footsteps," Joe whispered. "Maybe he'll lead us to the sword."

Frank hesitated for a moment. "What about Nancy? Maybe we should try to find her before that big guy does."

If you think Frank and Joe should try to find Nancy,
turn to page 23.
If you think Frank and Joe should follow the footsteps,
turn to page 28.

22

Nancy studied her road map of England as Frank pulled away from Simon Pethick's country house.

"The airfield is just south of here, on the coast," she said. "We should be able to reach it in forty-five minutes."

"We shouldn't be too far behind Simon Pethick," Joe said. "Keep a close watch on the map, Nancy. We can't afford to make a wrong turn."

Frank drove their rented car through the English countryside, carefully following Nancy's directions. As she predicted, they arrived at the Channel airfield in three-quarters of an hour.

"There's the control tower," Nancy announced. "Drop us off there, Frank."

As Frank parked the car, Nancy and Joe rushed into the building.

"Has a Mr. Simon Pethick been here today?" Nancy asked an official inside.

"Why, yes," the man replied. "He has received clearance for takeoff in ten minutes. I'm afraid you're too late to talk to him. That's his plane right there." The man pointed to a red-and-white Piper Cub taxiing onto the runway.

Turn to page 34.

23

Frank and Joe wound their way back through the maze, looking for Nancy. Suddenly, they came upon a small, thatched hut.

"Frank, look," Joe said to his brother as he examined the ground. "There was a struggle here between two people. And one set of footprints is smaller. Maybe they belong to Nancy."

Inside the hut, Nancy recognized Joe's voice.

"Joe, Frank," she tried to call out through the gag in her mouth.

The Hardy boys heard her muffled cry and forced open the latch on the door. Nancy stumbled out into the blinding sunlight, happy to see her friends.

"Who did this to you?" Joe demanded as he freed her from the ropes.

"A big, tall guy with a beard," Nancy explained. "He must be long gone by now, though."

Frank studied his diagram of the maze. "Let's follow this path a few more turns," he said. "My hunch is that we're close to something interesting."

Turn to page 46.

24

"A hidden staircase," Joe exclaimed. "That's how the person who pushed the statue escaped."

Frank pulled out a penlight from his shirt pocket and shone it into the dark passageway that had steps going both up and down.

The sleuths heard a soft thud in the passage above them. At the same time, they discerned what sounded like a muffled scream, coming from below.

"I'll check out the sound from above," Joe said.

"We'll see who needs help down these stairs," Frank added as he and Nancy began to descend the stairs in the passageway.

If you want to go with Joe, turn to page 29.
If you want to go with Frank and Nancy, turn to page 48.

Slowly, Nancy's eyes adjusted to the dim light of the hut. Her searching gaze fell upon several tools attached to one wall. She backed up and fumbled to reach a scythe that was hanging at the level of her waist. Once she found it, the young detective began to rub the ropes that were tied around her wrists against its sharp blade.

Soon she had freed herself and torn the gag from her mouth. I can't call out for help, Nancy thought. That brute might be the first to hear me.

Turn to page 27.

27

She tried the door, but it was latched tight, as she suspected. Then she picked up a rake and began to poke through the thatched roof of the hut. Dust and straw fell into her face, making her sneeze and cough. But after ten minutes of hard work, Nancy had made a hole large enough to climb through. She hoisted her agile body up into the opening and squinted her eyes in the bright sunlight.

"Now I have to get out of this maze," Nancy said to herself with determination. She reached for her map, but to her distress she found that it was gone. It must have fallen out of my pocket during the struggle with that big guy, she thought.

Turn to page 45.

28

"But then we'll lose the man!" Joe insisted. "Nancy knows how to take care of herself. Come on!"

"You're right," Frank agreed. "I just hope we can keep up with him."

The brothers cautiously crept along the path, following the sounds of the footsteps on the other side of the hedge. Frank continued to draw their route on his notepad.

"Oh, no!" Joe said with frustration as they came to a sharp right turn. "I can hear him going off to the left."

Frank studied his diagram.

"Look at this, Joe. My hunch is that if we turn right here, and then right again, we'll be out of here in another few minutes. And I'm sure the man is heading out, too."

Frank's prediction proved correct. Within a short time, the brothers emerged from the maze, facing a small forest.

"Frank, look!" Joe said excitedly. "Our guy is heading into those woods!" He pointed to a tall, heavyset man in a green outfit.

The boys hurried after the stranger, who disappeared among the trees.

Turn to page 60.

Joe crept up the narrow passageway. He soon came to a small wooden door that was slightly ajar.

This must be the attic over the top floor of the house, he thought to himself.

As Joe pushed open the creaking door, there was a scurrying sound in the room, followed by a crash.

Joe hesitated for a moment, and then entered the small, dimly lit attic. As he glanced at the rafters in the ceiling, he suddenly caught sight of two eerie, golden-green eyes.

Turn to page 30.

30

"Me-ow!" The shrill, frightened scream of a cat echoed through the attic.

Joe's tense muscles relaxed, and he began to chuckle. "Looks like all I caught is a cat burglar," he said.

The young sleuth lifted the frightened cat from the rafters and set it on the floor. Then he hurried down the passageway to rejoin his brother and Nancy.

Turn to page 48.

When Nancy, Mr. Drew, and the Hardy boys returned to their London hotel, they found a message from the police waiting for them.

"The owner of the car is a woman named Miss Natasha Berenski," Nancy explained as she read the message. "She lives at 40 Palace Gate."

"You could take a bus there," Mr. Drew informed her. "I have an important appointment this afternoon in north London, and I'll need the car."

"Let's talk to Miss Berenski right away," Frank said. "She may be able to give us a clue about the thief."

Ten minutes later, Nancy, Frank, and Joe caught a red, double-decker bus and settled into the front seats. They watched London whiz by outside the window as they traveled along the south side of Hyde Park before stopping at Palace Gate.

"What a lovely neighborhood," Nancy exclaimed as they hopped from the bus and walked down the wide street lined with pillared townhouses.

"There's number 40," Frank said, pointing to a large, three-story house. He lifted up the heavy brass knocker on the door and let it fall.

A young woman came out a few moments later. She studied the three sleuths with her large, brown eyes. "Yes?" she said in a thick, Eastern European accent. "What do you want?"

Turn to page 32.

32

"Are you Natasha Berenski?" Nancy asked.

"Yes."

The young detective introduced herself and the Hardy brothers. Then she explained that they were working with the police on a criminal case involving the theft of Miss Berenski's car.

"Could we come in?" Joe asked.

The young woman hesitated, then reluctantly invited them into the house. When everyone was seated, Frank asked. "Where was your car parked when it was stolen, Miss Berenski?"

"I had left it on a side street not far from here," she answered. "I have no idea who might have taken it."

Nancy watched as their hostess shifted uncomfortably in her chair. Just then, the telephone on a nearby table rang sharply. Nervously, Miss Berenski picked it up. "Yes," she said into the phone, "very good."

Frank held up a hand. "Is that the police? I need to talk with them."

The dark-eyed woman handed him the phone. The young detective jotted down notes as he spoke to the authorities. After he hung up, he excitedly told Nancy and Joe, "They've found the car abandoned near the river. The police are waiting for us to come and examine it."

Turn to page 33.

The three young detectives said good-bye to Miss Berenski and left the house.

"We have to hurry," Frank said eagerly. "There may be an important clue in the car."

Nancy was walking along quietly, deep in thought. "You two go ahead," she said to the boys. "I suspect that Natasha Berenski knows more than she is telling us. I want to follow up on a hunch of my own."

If you want to follow Frank and Joe, turn to page 51.
If you want to stay with Nancy, turn to page 54.

34

"What is his destination, please?" Nancy asked.

"He is flying across the English Channel," the official answered, "to Calais, France."

"What can we do now?" Joe asked, turning to Nancy.

"We'll follow him," Nancy replied with determination.

By the time Frank entered the control tower, Nancy had already arranged to rent a three-seater plane.

"It's fortunate that I brought my pilot's license," the young sleuth said. "We'll trail Simon Pethick to Calais."

As the three friends walked on the airfield toward their blue Cherokee plane, they saw Simon Pethick take off.

"Let's hurry," Nancy urged, dashing toward the rented aircraft. "We're cleared for takeoff in twelve minutes."

After making a safety check of the plane, the young pilot climbed into her seat. Frank and Joe strapped themselves in behind her.

Minutes later, they were airborne, heading east to cross the English Channel.

Turn to page 35.

Joe gazed down at the gray water below them.

"People actually swim across the English Channel," he said in amazement.

"Aren't you glad we're flying?" Nancy asked, glancing back at Joe with a twinkle in her eye.

"I can see the French coast already," Frank exclaimed, pointing out the window. "And there is Simon Pethick's plane, dropping its altitude."

Nancy checked her flight plan and then began her descent, trailing the red-and-white Piper Cub through the air. She picked up the radio receiver and called the Calais airfield for landing instructions.

"I'm glad you speak French, Nancy," Frank said with a chuckle.

"Moi, aussi," Nancy replied; "me, too."

The experienced young pilot brought the plane down on French soil in a perfect landing and taxied to a stop near Simon Pethick's Piper Cub.

"There he is," Joe cried out as he saw the solicitor hop from his Piper Cub. "And he's carrying a sword!"

Turn to page 43.

36

Nancy hurried out the bookstore after Natasha Berenski. When the young woman reached Cromwell Road, she jumped into a waiting bus. The bus pulled away just as Nancy came up to the busy road.

"I can't lose her now," the young detective whispered to herself in frustration.

Luckily, another bus pulled up a few seconds later. Nancy hopped on board and hurried to the front, keeping her eyes on the red bus ahead.

The two buses traveled east into the city, stopping to let off and take on passengers. At the edge of Green Park, Nancy saw Miss Berenski get off and walk briskly in the direction of Buckingham Palace.

Nancy jumped from her bus and followed the suspicious young woman through the park. Ten minutes later, they arrived at Buckingham Palace, home of the British royalty.

Turn to page 37.

The area was filled with tourists who had come to see the changing of the Queen's guard. Nancy wove in and out of the crowd, never losing sight of Natasha Berenski, who worked her way toward the black gate in front of the palace.

Soldiers dressed in red jackets, black trousers, and big, black hats were marching back and forth inside the gate. Others were posted at points nearby.

Nancy watched as Natasha Berenski walked up to one of the guards, and slipped a message to him. Quickly, he took the paper and hid it in his uniform.

Nancy studied the guard's face carefully, making sure she could identify him later. Then she hurried away from the crowd to find a telephone booth. The young sleuth dropped in a coin and dialed the number of her hotel.

"Fenton Hardy's room, please," she asked the operator. When the investigator came on the line, Nancy told him everything she had seen. He instructed her to meet him at 40 Palace Gate in one hour.

Turn to page 41.

38

Frank and Joe hurried to the nearest red telephone box and eagerly flipped through the pages of a London telephone book.

"She's listed, all right," Joe said with satisfaction. "Her address is 185 Ladbroke Grove. Let's go back to the hotel and meet Nancy. After dinner, we'll see what we can learn from Lady Merlina's crystal ball."

Turn to page 55.

39

"You're safe for now, Evan, but I stole that sword just in time," Simon Pethick warned. "Carson Drew, a lawyer from the States, came to Bromley Hall this morning. He must be looking for something."

"Maybe he came to examine my grandfather's business affairs," Evan Bromley replied. "I was smart enough to discover how you've been cheating the family all these years."

"We're even now," the solicitor said in a disgusted voice. "I've stolen the new will that would have disinherited you. You keep quiet about the money I took from your grandfather."

Nancy met Frank and Joe's gaze as they listened to the conversation. Then the three sleuths walked up to the cottage door and knocked. They heard a hushed, confused exchange between the men inside. Then Simon Pethick pulled open the door.

"What do you want?" he asked suspiciously as he recognized the young Americans from their encounter in the driveway of Bromley Hall. Evan Bromley heard the note of alarm in the solicitor's voice. He grabbed the paper from the coffee table and took off out the back door.

Turn to page 40.

40

"Joe, follow him," Frank cried out. "Nancy and I will stay here with Mr. Pethick."

Joe quickly circled around the cottage to the back. He arrived just as Evan Bromley jumped on one of the horses tethered there and rode off into a thick woods.

Without hesitation, Joe untethered and mounted another horse. He guided the chestnut mare down the trail after Evan Bromley.

Joe was an experienced rider, but he could see that Bromley was an accomplished equestrian as well. The young man was riding his black horse at a great speed down the bridle path, which was familiar to him.

Joe urged his mare to go faster. They galloped along the path that wound through the woods and into an open meadow.

As Joe drew closer to the fugitive, he shouted to the young man, "Give yourself up. We know all about the knight's sword!"

Evan Bromley cast a desperate look over his shoulder at Joe. Then he kicked his horse to go faster.

Turn to page 53.

Later that afternoon, Nancy met Fenton Hardy, Frank, and Joe near Natasha Berenski's house.

"I'm glad you phoned me, Nancy," Fenton Hardy said. "It sounds as though this case may involve national security. I want to question Miss Berenski myself."

As the four investigators started down the street to 40 Palace Gate, they saw a man come out of Miss Berenski's house.

"It's Jenkins!" Joe gasped, "the butler from Bromley Hall."

"Look at the package he's carrying," Frank said, pointing to the long, thin parcel in Jenkins's hand.

Seconds later, Jenkins recognized the sleuths. He whirled around and ran away from them.

Frank and Joe sped after the butler and stopped his escape. Fenton Hardy and Nancy reached them as Frank pulled the parcel from Jenkins's hands and began to unwrap it.

"A sword!" Nancy exclaimed, looking at Jenkins in surprise. "It must be the Silver Knight's."

Fenton Hardy pulled the butler toward his car, which was parked up the street. "We're going to the police," he told him. "You have a lot of things to explain."

Turn to page 42.

42

At the police station, the mystery of the knight's sword began to unravel. Jenkins confessed that he worked as an agent for a foreign spy ring in London. Lord Bromley himself had been a secret agent for the British government. Jenkins had learned that the knight's sword contained an important secret. He had helped Miss Berenski and her cohorts steal the sword. But they had not been able to find the hidden information.

"What about the guard at Buckingham Palace?" Nancy asked the butler.

"He was placed there as a spy," Jenkins answered. "We had the perfect set-up, until you interfered."

Meanwhile, Fenton Hardy had opened the knight's sword. He motioned Nancy, Frank, and Joe to come into another room.

"Lord Bromley's secret is safe," Mr. Hardy told the young sleuths. "The sword contained the names of top-level foreign spies in England. I'll turn over the information to the government."

"And tomorrow, we'll bring the sword back to Bromley Hall," Nancy said. Then she added with a laugh, "I'll bet the Silver Knight never knew he was working as a secret agent!"

END

The young detectives jumped from their blue Cherokee and ran toward Simon Pethick. A startled expression came over the man's face when he saw them. Frantically, he tried to hide the sword.

"Your game is over, Mr. Pethick," Frank warned sternly, reaching out. "Give me Lord Bromley's property."

The older man regained his composure and calmly handed the sword to Frank.

"You may see it, of course," he said. "But there must be some mistake. I am acting under Lord Bromley's instructions to sell the sword in France."

Frank handed it to Nancy, who immediately twisted off its hilt and pulled a paper from inside. The expression on Simon Pethick's face changed from confidence to panic.

"Give me that paper," he snarled at Nancy.

Joe and Frank restrained him as Nancy read the secret of the knight's sword.

Turn to page 44.

44

"Dear Mr. Drew," Nancy read. "I have reason to suspect that my trusted solicitor, Simon Pethick, has deceived and cheated me. Please conduct a thorough examination of my estate. If my suspicions are correct, have Mr. Pethick prosecuted to the full extent of the law. Lord Bromley."

After Nancy had finished reading, she looked up at Pethick's defiant face.

"What do you have to say for yourself, Mr. Pethick?" she asked.

The solicitor stared back at her arrogantly. "I have nothing to say to you, young woman. I'll save that for my legal counsel."

"Very well," Nancy replied. "Now I'll call Bromley Hall. Elizabeth will be delighted to learn that the knight's sword is safe. And," she added with a smile, "I'll have to let Dad know that we're having lunch in France!"

END

Nancy jumped down from the hut onto the ground. Nervously glancing over her shoulder to see if the burly man was following her, she crept back through the maze, trying to find a way out.

Suddenly, she came upon a small section of the hedge that had been hacked open. She stopped to examine the severed stems of the bushes.

"Whoever did this," she whispered to herself, "was in a hurry to get away. I wonder why?"

She stepped through the broken hedge and saw another opening a short distance away. Quickly, she ran to it and squeezed through, cutting her legs on the sharp stems.

The young detective ignored the pain as she realized with relief that she was now outside the maze. Ahead of her were the stables of Bromley Hall. Nancy started off to search them.

Turn to page 59.

46

The three sleuths followed the twisting maze for several more yards. A final sharp turn brought them into an eight-sided opening. At its center was a cast-iron replica of the Silver Knight standing on a four-foot base.

Frank walked straight up to it and looked at it closely. He noticed that there was a narrow crack between the bottom of the statue and its base.

"Hey, Joe, come help me move this," he said. "Maybe there's a hiding place underneath."

Joe lifted the statue on one side, Frank on the other. Cautiously, they lowered it to the ground.

Nancy looked curiously into the hollow area that was now exposed. Then she cried out in surprise.

"What's the matter?" Frank asked.

"Well—there's a silver sword in the base," Nancy replied. "I'll bet it's the one we're looking for. But— there's a nasty-looking snake wound around it!"

Turn to page 47.

Frank and Joe cautiously peered into the base. They, too, saw the thick, black snake that had coiled itself around the sword's hilt.

"I have an idea," Frank said. "Pull two strong branches from the hedge and strip off their leaves. We'll use them to get the snake off and lift out the sword."

Nancy and Joe followed his instructions. Then Frank took one stick and handed the other to his brother. Nancy watched as the Hardys worked to separate the snake from the sword. Finally, Joe triumphantly pulled the weapon out of the base while Frank held down the snake with his branch.

Joe quickly handed Nancy the sword and then the boys lifted the statue back into place.

"Whew!" Frank said, wiping his forehead. "I never want to see that reptile again."

Meanwhile, Nancy followed Lord Bromley's instructions to open the sword. As she twisted off the hilt, a piece of parchment fell to the ground.

"This is it," she said as she picked up the paper. "Lord Bromley's secret."

Turn to page 88.

48

"Someone needs our help," Frank said, flashing his penlight into the narrow, hidden passageway that descended inside the walls of the house.

"Let's hurry," Nancy urged.

Frank led the way down the steep, creaking stairs. The two young detectives had to push away cobwebs that caught on their faces as they went.

"Wait for me," Joe called out from above them. "I didn't find anything important up the stairs."

As the sleuths went lower and lower in the passage, they noticed that the air had a damp, musty smell.

"We're at the end," Frank said suddenly, as the beam of his penlight shone on an old wooden door at the bottom of the staircase.

A few seconds later, his foot pushed against something soft on the steps. He flashed his light down to examine what it was.

"It's Elizabeth!" Nancy gasped, stooping over the silent form of the young woman.

Turn to page 50.

50

Elizabeth's eyelids fluttered as she heard Nancy's voice. At first, she opened her mouth to scream, but then she recognized the young detectives.

"I must have fainted," she murmured drowsily. "I thought you were Jenkins at first. I was afraid he had come back to get me."

"Jenkins!" Nancy said in a surprised whisper. "Did he put you in here?"

"Yes," Elizabeth replied. "Philip had to leave for an important meeting in London. When I left him at the door, I saw Jenkins sneaking down the stairs off the hallway into the cellar. I followed him, and he grabbed me. He put something over my mouth to make me faint. I think I screamed before I passed out."

"We heard you," Frank assured her. "Where is Jenkins now?"

Elizabeth pointed to the wooden door. "I suspect he's still in the old cellar."

Turn to page 63.

Frank and Joe arrived at the address the police had given them, a narrow alley near the Thames River. Two English bobbies and a detective were waiting for them beside the abandoned green Ford.

"I'm Frank Hardy and this is my brother Joe," Frank said, shaking hands with the policemen.

"I'm Detective Holdaway," the detective said warmly. "I've met your father. We're glad to have members of the Hardy family working with us on this case."

"Did you find anything of interest in the car?" Joe asked, slipping into the front seat.

"We searched the seats and the trunk and found nothing," the detective said. "In the glove compartment, there are several books and papers belonging to Miss Berenski, I believe."

Joe popped open the glove compartment and glanced through the material inside. His attention was caught by a tour book about London, which was dog-eared and grubby.

"Miss Berenski didn't seem like the type to treat a book like this," he said to Frank as he flicked through the pages. In the middle of the volume, he found a yellowed business card.

Turn to page 52.

52

Printed on it were the words:

LADY MERLINA

FORTUNE TELLER

Underneath was a picture of a crystal ball.

As Joe started to take the card from the book, Frank suddenly grabbed his hand. "Look at the pages the card is between! They contain a description of the Tower of London, and the words *The Armory* are underlined."

"And there's a date in the margin," Joe added. "It's today's!"

"It could mean two things," Frank said. "Either someone has planned a sightseeing trip to the Tower today, or—something more sinister."

"We may have found two good clues," Joe said. "Which should we follow up first?"

If you think Frank and Joe should investigate Lady Merlina, turn back to page 38.
If you think they should go to the Tower of London, turn to page 65.

Ahead of them, Joe saw a high hedge. He reined in his mare, not knowing the horse well enough to make the jump. Evan Bromley braced himself to fly over the treacherous hurdle.

Joe watched as the black horse and its rider sailed into the air and over the hedge. Then, from the other side, he heard a frightened whinny followed by the dull thud of a body hitting the ground.

Hastily, Joe guided his mount to an opening in the hedge a quarter of a mile away. As he came out on the other side, he saw Evan Bromley sprawled on the ground and his horse galloping away in the distance.

"My leg," the young man moaned as Joe came up to him. "It must be broken."

"Hand over the will," Joe ordered as he dismounted. "Then I'll go for help."

Evan Bromley knew he was defeated. He pulled a parchment paper from his riding breeches.

"I didn't steal this," he whined. "Simon Pethick did. He's the one who will have to go to jail."

Joe gazed down at Lord Bromley's grandson. "Your grandfather was right about you," he said, taking the document. "You don't deserve to inherit Bromley Hall."

END

54

After Frank and Joe left, Nancy searched for a place from where she could spy on the house of Natasha Berenski. She found an old bookshop nearby and browsed through the shelves near its front windows.

A short time later, Nancy saw a man hurrying down the street toward 40 Palace Gate. He opened the door of the house without knocking and went inside.

"Could I help you find a book, miss?" a sales clerk asked Nancy politely.

"No, not today," she replied. "I'm just looking."

She continued to peer out the window, keeping a close watch on the house. Ten minutes later, both Miss Berenski and the man walked out onto the street. They carried on a short conversation and then parted, going off in different directions.

I wonder which one I should follow? Nancy thought to herself as she emerged from the book-store.

If you think Nancy should follow the young woman, turn back to page 36.
If you think Nancy should follow the man, turn to page 58.

55

In the dim twilight, Nancy glanced at the peeling paint on the door of 185 Ladbroke Grove. Then she calmly pushed the buzzer after checking her watch. She had arrived exactly on time for her appointment with Lady Merlina. Behind her, hidden in the thick shrubbery, were Frank and Joe.

The old door suddenly creaked open, revealing a large woman in gypsy dress.

"I am Lady Merlina," she announced. "You must be Miss Drew."

"Yes . . . yes, that's right," Nancy answered, acting nervous. "I want you to tell my fortune."

"Come in, then, dearie, come in," Lady Merlina whispered, giving Nancy a gold-toothed, knowing smile.

Nancy followed the woman into a small room with thick drapes covering the windows. Lady Merlina sat down and motioned for Nancy to sit across from her. Between them was a large, weirdly lit crystal ball.

"Now, dearie, what is it you want to know?" the gypsy asked. "Is it your love life?"

Out of the corner of her eyes, Nancy saw Frank and Joe sneak through the hallway of Lady Merlina's house.

Turn to page 56.

56

"Yes, my love life," Nancy whispered dramatically to the fortune teller.

Lady Merlina gazed into her crystal ball. Then she closed her eyes, appearing to go into a trance.

The hushed atmosphere of the room was suddenly broken by a man's yell and loud scuffling from the next room.

Nancy jumped from her chair and ran to the doorway. "Don't try to go anywhere, Lady Merlina," she warned the fortune teller.

A moment later, Frank and Joe came into the room, dragging a young man with them.

"Ramón," the woman shouted at him. "What trouble have you got us into!"

"Be quiet, Mama," the young man shouted back to her.

"We found Ramón in the next room," Frank explained, "along with a stash of valuable articles. They're all antiques, like the sword of the Silver Knight."

"Oh, that sword!" Lady Merlina moaned. "I knew it would get us into trouble." She turned to the young detectives. "I'll tell you anything you want to know. Just don't contact the police, please. I don't want my Ramón back in jail."

Turn to page 57.

"What do you know?" Frank asked, promising nothing.

"A week ago, a rich man came to me. He offered me a large amount of money if Ramón and I would put a curse on Bromley Hall. He said all we had to do was steal the sword of the Silver Knight."

"Tell us where the sword is now," Joe said threateningly.

"Felix Hume has it," Lady Merlina said, "the man who paid us to steal it. He lives on Eaton Place, 66 Eaton Place."

Frank and Joe released Ramón, who gave them an evil, cunning grin.

"You will be hearing from the authorities," Joe said as the detectives started to leave.

After they had walked out of the house, Nancy turned to Joe. "Why did you warn him about the police? He might try to get away."

"That's exactly what I want him to do," Joe said. "I'll stay here to follow his trail. You and Frank drive back to the hotel and contact Detective Holdaway."

"Then we'll go to Eaton Place," Nancy said. "I want to find out more about Mr. Felix Hume."

If you want to stay with Joe and follow Ramón, turn to page 66.

If you want to go with Frank and Nancy to Eaton Place, turn to page 77.

58

Nancy hurried to catch the light as she saw the man cross Kensington High Street and go into the park. She followed him down a walk that went north through the park. Soon, the walk joined another path that wound along the Serpentine, a river filled with rowboats and water birds.

What a perfect day to go boating, Nancy thought. She promised herself that she'd come back to the Serpentine when the knight's sword had been found.

Enough people were in the park to allow her to follow the man undetected as he hurried to its northern end. She kept his brown jacket in sight as he darted out of the park and across a main street into the business area of the city.

She saw a sign with an arrow pointing in the direction he was headed. It read PADDINGTON STATION. The young sleuth smiled to herself as she remembered the rail ticket that Frank and Joe had found on the grounds of Bromley Hall.

Turn to page 70.

Stealthily, Nancy crept up to the stables and peered through the door. From the third stall came the frightened whinny of a chestnut mare. Nancy stepped inside, wondering what had alarmed the animal.

Suddenly, the burly man who had locked her in the hut before jumped from behind the second stall, holding a sword tightly in both hands. "So you're still snooping around, are you, young lady?" he asked. He pointed the tip of the weapon at Nancy with a threatening sneer. "If it's Lord Bromley's sword that you're after, you're out of luck. I'm not going to be so easy on you this time."

Nancy stood her ground, intently watching the chestnut mare, who now was moving up behind her assailant. The horse suddenly reared up and struck the man in the back with his front hooves. He sprawled out on the floor at Nancy's feet, knocked unconscious, and the silver sword flew from his hands.

Its sharp point dug into the ground near the stable doorway and stuck there, shining brilliantly, as Frank and Joe arrived on the scene.

Turn to page 86.

60

A few moments later, the boys caught sight of the man again, who was awkwardly darting through the underbrush.

"He's carrying a sword!" Frank said as they were gaining on him.

Joe nodded. "He's also pretty old. I saw his face when he looked back."

Just then, the green-clad figure stopped running and hid behind a thick tree trunk. The Hardys slowed down and advanced cautiously.

Suddenly, with a dramatic gesture, the man jumped from behind the tree, waving the sword in the air.

"Robin Hood demands that you leave Sherwood Forest," he proclaimed, straightening the green cap on his gray head.

"Robin Hood?" Joe asked in disbelief.

"Aye, Robin Hood," the man answered shakily. "I've had a hard day stealing from the rich to give to the poor."

Frank and Joe looked at each other in amusement. Joe twirled the green feather that he had found in the hedge.

"Perhaps this is yours, Robin."

"Thank you, lad," the man said as he took the feather and stuck it in his cap. "You're invited to join my merry men."

Turn to page 62.

62

"We want to take that sword back to its rightful owners," Frank said, firmly reaching out to take the weapon.

Reluctantly, Robin handed it to him. "I guess you're right," he mumbled. "The Silver Knight needs his sword."

"And you'd better come with us," Joe said, taking the man's arm. "I wouldn't want to try to explain this without you."

Turn to page 94.

Frank helped Elizabeth to her feet. Then he cautiously turned the knob on the old, wooden door.

It swung open quietly, revealing the candlelit cellar of Bromley Hall. At the far end, Frank saw Jenkins, bent over a table with his back to them. He seemed to be working feverishly at something.

Frank motioned Joe and Nancy to follow as he stealthily crept from the hidden passage across the floor. When the three sleuths were only a few yards away from the butler, he suddenly whirled around and faced them. In his hand, he held a sword!

The light from a nearby candle flickered over his frightened, perspiring face.

"Why did you have to show up here this morning?" he whimpered pathetically. "I had it all planned. I was going to disappear from Bromley Hall tonight with the Silver Knight's sword. Why did you have to ruin everything!"

"Hand me the sword," Frank demanded.

Turn to page 64.

64

"But I haven't found the secret yet," Jenkins said frantically. "I guessed that Lord Bromley had hidden something inside the sword before he died. I could have been a rich man instead of a butler if you hadn't caught me."

Frank stepped toward the man to take the weapon. Suddenly, Jenkins raised it threateningly and pointed it at the young detective.

At that moment, Elizabeth moved forward into the glow of the candlelight.

"Give me the sword, Jenkins," she ordered bravely.

The butler's courage crumbled. He threw the sword to the ground and ran for the stairs. Joe and Frank started after him.

"No, let him go," Elizabeth pleaded. "He betrayed the family, but I don't want to prosecute him. His dismissal from Bromley Hall will be punishment enough. Now," she added, "it's time to learn my grandfather's secret."

Turn to page 102.

An hour later, Frank and Joe stood in the Armory of the Tower of London. The building contained the most famous weapons and suits of armor in British history.

"Look at this awful axe," Joe said to his brother. "It was used to behead prisoners."

Frank nodded glumly. Then he pointed to a richly carved set of armor. "That belonged to Henry VIII. Pretty fancy, isn't it?"

"All this must be worth a fortune!" Joe exclaimed, his eyes sweeping around the room.

"Yes, it *is* worth a fortune," a man's voice said from behind them. "That's why we're so worried about it."

Frank and Joe turned to face the portly gentleman who had spoken to them.

"I'm Timothy Morgan," he said, "the curator of the Armory. Detective Holdaway rang up to tell me you were coming."

"We're following a lead on a sword missing from Bromley Hall," Frank explained.

"That's not the only sword that's missing," Mr. Morgan said. "The police told us that similar thefts have taken place recently throughout England. A great number of fine swords and other old weapons have been stolen."

Frank and Joe looked at the man in surprise.

Turn to page 76.

66

Joe had been right about Ramón. A short time after the sleuths left the house, Lady Merlina's son hurried out the door, carrying a large canvas bag. He jumped into a car and sped away.

Joe hopped into a taxi and instructed the driver to follow Ramón who was traveling through London to the east. Joe's cab followed him across the Thames River to the South Bank where Ramón suddenly stopped.

As Joe paid his driver, the man warned him, "Be careful in this part of London at night. You might meet a bad bloke in an alleyway."

Joe thanked him for the advice, then he hurried after Ramón, who had left his car and walked down a narrow street into darkness. Joe surveyed the area as he trailed his suspect. It was an old section of London with dilapidated, empty warehouses. He cautiously followed the sound of Ramón's footsteps. Occasionally, he caught a glimpse of the man's figure in the moonlight.

Suddenly, a large rat scurried past him in the alley, rubbing against his leg. With a muffled cry, Joe jumped aside, almost giving himself away. But Ramón did not look back. He turned a corner and entered an old pub. Its wooden sign read: THE BLACK PARROT.

Turn to page 67.

Joe stepped into the pub a few moments later. It was dimly lit by golden-colored lamps. He saw Ramón slip through the crowd of people and go through a door at the back. The young detective felt fairly certain that the man hadn't seen him. But he also knew that he was in dangerous and unfamiliar territory. He looked at the telephone hanging on the wall. It would be safer for him to see if he could reach Frank and Nancy at the hotel and tell them where he was. But if he did, he might lose Ramón's trail.

67

If you think Joe telephoned Frank and Nancy, turn to page 68; then wait for further instructions.
If you think Joe should follow Ramón immediately, turn to page 68; then wait for further instructions.

68

Joe worked his way through the crowd of people in the pub to the door at the back. Looking around to see if anyone was watching, he opened it quickly and slipped through, closing it quietly behind him. He found himself at the top of a flight of rickety steps leading into an old cellar.

Joe waited until his eyes adjusted to the dim light. He could hear two men talking in the room below. Stealthily, he crept toward the bottom steps until he spied Ramón standing at a table with another man. The table was spread with loot.

"Good work, Ramón," the swarthy, older man said in an oily voice. "I'll be able to find buyers in America for this haul with no trouble at all."

Joe gasped as he saw that the swarthy man was examining a sword made of carved silver. Just as I suspected, Joe thought to himself, Ramón never gave the sword to Felix Hume. He hoped to sell it.

"I've handled swords like this one before," the criminal said. "Sometimes the hilt has a secret hiding place."

Joe held his breath as the man tried to twist off the hilt. To the boy's dismay, he succeeded. As it separated from the sword, a red velvet bag dropped from inside. Greedily, the criminal pulled on its drawstring. . . .

Turn to page 69.

The contents of the bag fell into the criminal's dirty hand. "My, my, my," he said gloatingly, "what a fine treasure to add to my collection." He held up the beautiful diamond necklace that Lord Bromley had hidden in the knight's sword.

Ramón stared at the necklace jealously. "That's as much mine as it is yours, Lopez," he said.

"Don't be ridiculous," the man snarled. "I've already paid you for the work you've done."

Joe crept down another step to get a better view. But the old board suddenly gave way under him, and the young detective sprawled down the steps onto the cellar floor!

The two thieves rushed to grab him. Ramón twisted his arms back, then Lopez bound his wrists together.

"Whoever you are," he sneered at Joe, "you'll be taking an unexpected trip."

If you had Joe telephone Frank and Nancy, turn to page 80.

If you didn't have Joe telephone Frank and Nancy, turn to page 99.

70

The man entered Paddington Station. Nancy walked up closer so she wouldn't lose him in the crowd. He suddenly stopped in front of a wall of tall, narrow lockers and pulled a key from his pocket. Nancy lingered beside a train map, watching him.

The man opened the locker, looked quickly inside, and then slammed it shut again. Then he walked briskly away, heading for the exit of the station.

Nancy trained her eye on the locker the man had opened, and walked close enough to read its number.

"Three-six-four," she murmured to herself. "I wonder what's inside?"

Then she turned to catch sight of the man, who was just going out the door of Paddington Station.

If you think Nancy should investigate the contents of the locker, turn to page 71.
If you think she should follow the man again, turn to page 72.

Nancy decided to find out what was in the locker rather than follow the man. As she looked around to find a policeman, she was startled by the sight of a familiar face. "Mr. Hardy!" she gasped. "I didn't expect to see you here!"

The detective smiled. "And I was curious as to why you were following Vladimir Kurpov."

"You know that man?" Nancy asked in surprise.

"Yes, I do," Mr. Hardy replied. "He is part of a spy ring I am investigating for the British government. Now tell me what you know."

Nancy explained about the theft of the knight's sword and her investigation of Natasha Berenski.

"I'll have to get in touch with government security immediately," Fenton Hardy said. "And you must remain perfectly silent about all you know, Nancy."

The girl nodded in agreement as she followed Mr. Hardy to a telephone booth.

"Wait out here for me," Mr. Hardy said.

Turn to page 74.

72

Nancy decided to return to the locker later. She was more curious about where the mysterious man might go next.

The young sleuth hurried toward the door he had gone through, and emerged on a busy street in front of Paddington Station. To her dismay, the stranger was nowhere in sight.

Suddenly, Nancy felt a strong arm circle her shoulder.

"Don't make a sound," a man's voice hissed in her ear, "or you'll be sorry."

Before she could struggle from his grip, Nancy was pushed into the back seat of a waiting car.

Turn to page 85.

73

As the three young detectives emerged from the shaded drive, they saw a breathtaking sight. Before them stood an ancient castle, its towers and turrets outlined against the moonlit sky. A moat encircled the building, making it unreachable except by a drawbridge that stretched over the water.

"I don't see our man anywhere," Joe whispered. "He must have driven right into the castle."

"Let's get across while the bridge is still down," Frank whispered back. "I don't see any lights except on the top floor. That gives us a good chance of not being seen."

Joe and Nancy followed Frank's lead across the drawbridge. When they reached its end, they cautiously crept into the courtyard of the castle.

Suddenly, from behind them, they heard the loud creaking of wood. They whirled around to see the span being raised.

Then, from the courtyard, they heard a wicked cackle. A second later, a match flared in the darkness, and a lantern was lit. In the glow of the light, the sleuths stared into the evil face of an old man. He was clad in a long, velvet robe.

Turn to page 107.

74

When Fenton Hardy finished his call, he rejoined Nancy.

"I just learned some rather startling news," the investigator told her. "Lord Bromley worked as a secret agent for the British government for many years. The official I spoke with believes that the secret he wrote your father about may involve classified information. They suggest that we get into the locker before someone else does."

After obtaining a master key to locker 364 from the station's security chief, Fenton Hardy and Nancy went to open the tall, narrow locker. Mr. Hardy reached inside and pulled out a long, thin parcel wrapped in brown paper. He tore off a piece of the wrapping, revealing a sword's hilt with a lion carved in it.

"The Silver Knight's sword!" Nancy exclaimed.

"Let's take it to the hotel," Fenton Hardy said as he closed the locker door. "I want to open it in private."

Frank and Joe had already returned to the hotel and joined Nancy and their father in his room. The investigator explained the events of the day.

"I had begun my surveillance of Natasha Berenski's house today before Kurpov came to see her. To my surprise, Nancy followed his trail to Paddington Station just ahead of me. I believe that he planned to remove the sword from the locker where he had stashed it earlier after stealing it from Bromley Hall. But, after noticing that Nancy had trailed him into the station, he changed his mind."

Turn to page 75.

"How is Natasha Berenski connected with the spy ring?" Frank asked his father.

"She works as a cultural attaché for an embassy in London," the investigator replied. "But that is only a front for her spy activities. Now, I want to open the sword."

Fenton Hardy twisted off the hilt and caught a roll of microfilm that tumbled out. "I'll process this immediately," he said as he took out the developing equipment that he had in his suitcase. Then he disappeared into the closet.

Frank and Joe, meanwhile, congratulated Nancy on her suspicion of Natasha Berenski. "You had the right idea!" Joe said admiringly.

"Well, I knew she wasn't reacting normally to the theft of her car," the sleuth explained. "She didn't seem upset enough."

Several minutes later, Fenton Hardy stepped back into the room, with a broad smile on his face. "I'll have to go and see the secret service people right away," he explained. "Lord Bromley uncovered very important information just before his death. Meanwhile, would you return the sword to Elizabeth, please?"

"We'll be glad to," Joe said. "And I'm sure she'll be more than glad to have it back!"

END

76

"That's right." Mr. Morgan nodded worriedly. "I've lost a lot of sleep wondering if someone will try to break in here. The guards get very nervous at night. Rumors are even circulating that the ghosts of the Tower are roaming about once again."

Frank told Mr. Morgan about the clue that had brought them to the Tower. Then he carefully surveyed the main room of the Armory. "I have an idea," he said. "Could we come here tonight with a friend of ours to back up the guards?"

"Why, yes," the curator replied. "Eleven o'clock would be a good time. That's when the late shift starts. We're a little short-handed then."

"Joe and I will conceal ourselves behind those heavy drapes," Frank explained, pointing to a large window. "If the thieves try to steal something, we'll surprise them."

"All right," Mr. Morgan agreed. "The guards will let you in at eleven."

Turn to page 83.

Nancy and Frank went back to the hotel and called the police, informing them about Lady Merlina and her son. Next, Nancy phoned Bromley Hall. Elizabeth told her that Felix Hume had been her grandfather's business partner in a South African diamond mine.

"Diamonds," Frank mused. "That would be a powerful motive for a crime."

A short time later, the two sleuths drove through Hyde Park, heading for Eaton Place, London's most elegant residential area.

"Perhaps Lady Merlina was bluffing," Frank said as he looked up at the grand house that was number 66. "This doesn't look like the hideout of a thief."

Nancy shrugged. "Let's find out."

The young detectives walked up the marble stairs of the house and rang the bell. A servant in formal dress opened the door.

"We'd like to speak with Mr. Felix Hume, please," Frank announced. "It's in reference to the Silver Knight."

"I'm afraid Mr. Hume is just leaving," the servant responded, "for South Africa."

"It's very important that we see him," Frank insisted, stepping inside. His keen eyes searched the hallway as Nancy kept the servant busy with conversation.

Turn to page 78.

78

To his amazement, Frank saw a silver sword lying on a desk in the library off the hall. It had a lion carved on its hilt! Frank gasped. This might be the sword we're looking for! he thought.

Seconds later, a tall, thin man with a twirled mustache appeared at the library door. "Come in here, young man," he demanded. When he saw Nancy, he motioned her inside as well. The servant closed the library door tightly behind them.

"I am Felix Hume," the tall man announced. "Who are you and what do you know about the Silver Knight?"

"We know that you had its sword stolen from Bromley Hall," Nancy said calmly.

"I think you know too much," Felix Hume said in a cold, cruel voice. "But only I know the secret inside the sword. Lord Bromley had found a new diamond mine in South Africa. It was to be a surprise for his family after his death."

Frank and Nancy watched anxiously as the tall, thin man began to pace back and forth, rubbing his hands together.

"Now all I have to do is get rid of the two of you. It shouldn't be too difficult to arrange the disappearance of two young Americans in a city as large as London."

Turn to page 79.

Suddenly, the door to the library was kicked open. "Stay right there, Hume," the stern voice of a London bobby ordered.

Nancy and Frank smiled at each other in relief.

"It's a good thing you mentioned to the police that we were coming here, Nancy," Frank said. Then he turned to Felix Hume. "Where is the information about the diamond mine, Mr. Hume?"

Felix Hume knew his dangerous game was over. He opened a desk drawer and handed Frank the documents that had been hidden inside the Silver Knight's sword.

"I'll call Elizabeth right now," Frank said, reaching for the telephone. "The sword of the Silver Knight will soon be back in Bromley Hall. And its secret will make Elizabeth a very rich young woman."

END

80

Joe knew he was in deep trouble. He tried to stall for time. "Wait until your mother finds out about the necklace, Ramón," he said. "She'll be furious with you for letting it get away."

"How do you know about Lady Merlina?" Lopez demanded.

"I met her at her house," Joe said. "From there Ramón led me right to you."

"You stupid fool," the man snarled at Ramón. "Let's get out of here."

Joe resisted with all his might when the two criminals tried to drag him from the cellar. It took them five minutes to force the young detective up the stairs and out into an alleyway. Only after Ramón landed a brutal punch in Joe's face did he decide he would have to cooperate with them.

As his two captors shoved him through the dark alley alongside the pub, Joe anxiously glanced over his shoulder. He wondered if he would ever see his brother and Nancy again.

Turn to page 81.

A short time later, Joe heard the lapping of water in the darkness. Lopez pushed him out of the alleyway onto a dock of the Thames River where a small boat was waiting for them.

"Watch him while I stash this loot in the hold," the older man ordered Ramón. Then he boarded the boat and disappeared down the steps.

Joe turned to look at his captor just as his brother Frank leaped from the shadows of the alley. The older Hardy pounced on Ramón and covered his mouth with his hand. A second later, Nancy appeared and freed Joe from the ropes around his wrists.

"It's good to see you two again!" Joe whispered with relief. "I'll take care of Ramón's buddy now. He's down in the hold."

He crept aboard the boat while Frank gagged Ramón and tied him up. As Lopez came up the steps, Joe landed a kick in his chest that sent him sprawling down again. After a brief struggle, Joe overpowered the man and tied him up. Then he locked him in the hold.

Turn to page 82.

82

When Joe reappeared, carrying the knight's sword and the diamond necklace, Nancy and Frank were waiting on the deck.

"Lopez found this inside the sword," the boy explained, holding the beautiful necklace up to the moonlight.

"Good work, Joe!" Nancy said admiringly.

"You were lucky you still caught us at the hotel when you called," Frank said to his brother. "Otherwise, you might have ended up at the bottom of the river."

END

At eleven o'clock that night, Frank, Joe, and Nancy parked near the Tower of London.

"I'll stay in the car," Nancy reiterated their strategy, "unless there is something suspicious I have to investigate."

"Right," Frank said. "One of us will come out at midnight and check with you."

"I hope we'll catch the thieves," Nancy said worriedly. "I spoke with Elizabeth this afternoon. She thinks the curse on Bromley Hall is really coming true. Lord Bromley's lawyer told her today that the family is in terrible debt. They may have to sell Bromley Hall."

"Well, with some luck we'll be able to prevent that," Joe said. "But now we'd better get inside the Tower." The two brothers stepped from the car and walked into the huge gray fortress. At night, it seemed like a sinister place with its old cells and torture rooms. The boys quickly made their way to the Armory, where a guard let them in.

Turn to page 84.

84

The thick drapes had been pulled over the window in the main room, which was well lit for security.

"We'll hide behind them if we hear anything suspicious," Frank told his brother. "But for now, we'll just wait out here."

Almost an hour had passed when Joe suddenly whispered to Frank, "Did you hear that? I think someone groaned near the door."

"Get behind the drapes, quick," Frank whispered back.

The sleuths slipped into their hiding place just in time. As they peeked through the opening between the drapes, they saw a terrifying sight. A huge man entered the room. His face was concealed by a black hood that had two eye slits.

The boys watched as the man pulled several swords and a black executioner's axe from an open case. Frank stared at his younger brother and saw real fear in Joe's eyes. The huge man seemed too big even for both the Hardy boys to handle!

If you think Frank and Joe should try to stop the thief now, turn to page 89.

If you think they should follow him later, turn to page 92.

From page 72

At ten o'clock that night, Joe and Frank Hardy returned to their hotel after investigating the stolen car.

"A message for you," a man at the desk called to them as they walked through the lobby.

Joe took the plain envelope the clerk handed to him and tore it open. "Frank, it's about Nancy," he exclaimed. "Here's what it says:

"LOOK ON THE SERPENTINE TONIGHT FOR YOUR FRIEND, NANCY DREW. THEN FORGET EVERYTHING YOU KNOW ABOUT THE KNIGHT'S SWORD. THIS IS YOUR ONLY WARNING."

Frank and Joe exchanged worried glances. Then they ran out of the hotel toward Hyde Park.

Turn to page 103.

86

Nancy smiled as she saw the amazed looks on the Hardy brothers' faces.

"Where have you two been?" she asked. "Lost in a maze?"

"We wondered if a certain damsel might be in distress," Joe said jokingly.

"But it looks as though you don't need two knights in shining armor." Frank laughed.

"Actually, I was saved by a horse!" Nancy said and explained what had happened. Then the three sleuths bent to examine the sword of the Silver Knight. On its hilt was an intricately carved lion with a sapphire eye.

"Press the lion's eye," Nancy recited the instructions as she pushed her thumb against the sapphire, "and twist the hilt to the right."

When she turned the hilt, it came off the sword and a parchment paper fell out onto her lap.

Just then, Carson Drew and Elizabeth rushed into the stable.

"Thank goodness you're all right, Nancy," Mr. Drew said with relief. "And you've found the sword!"

Elizabeth looked at the burly man who was beginning to groan as he regained consciousness. "That's the groom we fired last week because he was too cruel to the horses!" she exclaimed. "He must have stolen the sword out of spite."

Continue on to page 87.

"You see," the young woman went on, "Philip told me he had followed a suspicious man into the maze. But he lost him. We also found out that the falling statue was an accident. A maid saw my Doberman knock it over."

While Elizabeth talked, Nancy carefully unfolded the paper that held the secret of the knight's sword. A broad smile spread over her face as she looked at it. Then she handed the piece of parchment to her father. "Here, Dad." Mr. Drew took the paper and read it aloud.

" 'THE BROMLEY FAMILY OWES A GREAT DEBT TO THE DESCENDANTS OF RUSSELL DREW, WHO SAVED MY FATHER'S LIFE DURING WORLD WAR I. TO HIS SON, CARSON, AND HIS GRAND-DAUGHTER, NANCY, I BEQUEATH A PART OF MY VALUABLE LIBRARY, INCLUDING A RARE SET OF *THE ADVENTURES OF SHERLOCK HOLMES.*' "

"What a fitting gift!" Elizabeth exclaimed in delight. "Grandfather often said that he wanted to repay the Drew family."

"Well, Sherlock," Joe said to Nancy with a teasing smile. "Let's get this sword back where it belongs."

END

88

Frank and Joe waited eagerly as Nancy began to read Lord Bromley's letter.

"MY GRANDDAUGHTER, ELIZABETH, PLANS TO MARRY A MAN NAMED PHILIP HARRINGTON. I HAVE LEARNED THAT HE IS AN IMPOSTOR WHO HOPES TO STEAL MY GRANDDAUGHTER'S INHERITANCE. HIS REAL NAME IS PHILIPPE ARNOLDE. HE HAS BEEN CONVICTED OF THEFT AND BRIBERY IN FRANCE. BECAUSE I AM TOO ILL TO BREAK THIS NEWS TO ELIZABETH, I WANT YOU, CARSON DREW, TO SAVE THE BROMLEY FAMILY FROM THIS DISGRACE."

As Nancy refolded the letter, a look of anger flashed in her eyes. "So it was Philip who stole the sword. He must have learned that it contained secret information. But he didn't know how to find it," she reasoned.

"Let's get back to the house right away," Joe said, picking up the sword.

The three sleuths hurried through the twisting maze to the opening where they had entered.

As they walked away from the hedge toward Bromley Hall, they saw Philip leaving the house and hurrying toward his red sports car in the driveway.

"Nancy, you take the sword back to Elizabeth," Joe said. "Come on, Frank, let's catch that creep before he gets away."

If you want to follow Joe and Frank, turn to page 96.
If you want to follow Nancy, turn to page 98.

89

The boys waited until the man had turned his back to them and was busy stealing another sword from a case. Then they slipped from behind the curtains and crept to a nearby wall where two crossed rapiers were mounted. Frank pulled one down for himself and the other for his brother. The noise apparently alerted the thief, who suddenly whirled around. His evil eyes glared at the Hardys through the slits in his black hood.

"Fools!" he hissed, "you can't stop me!" He dropped all the weapons he held except the curved executioner's axe. Then he lunged at the boys, swinging the axe through the air.

Turn to page 91.

The Hardys were expert fencers, but the man was no ordinary foe. He was quick for his huge build and seemed fearless. Frank and Joe dodged away as his axe cut through the air near them.

For long minutes, the boys parried with the man, feeling as though they were doing a dance with death. They knew that with one swing of the axe, the executioner could mortally wound them.

Finally, Frank saw an opening. He flicked his rapier at the man, slicing into the hand that held the axe. With a scream of pain, the man dropped his axe. Within seconds, both Hardy brothers had their swords pointed at his chest.

"Guard, we need help," Joe screamed at the top of his lungs.

A moment later, police swarmed into the Armory. While two officers handcuffed the prisoner, a third spoke to the Hardy boys.

"We were alerted by a young lady that a hooded man climbed over the wall outside," he said. "Apparently, we were just in time. The intruder knocked out the guard in his path."

Turn to page 115.

92

While Frank and Joe were planning their next move, the huge man grabbed one more sword, then suddenly turned and hurried from the room! The two boys came out from their hiding place.

"Quick, we have to follow him," Frank whispered to Joe.

The brothers ran out the door and down the dark stairway. Suddenly, Frank stumbled over the lifeless form of a man and fell. Joe was too close behind to stop himself, and both boys and the man rolled down the rest of the steps.

Frank gingerly picked himself up. "Are you all right, Joe?" he asked.

Joe felt his head. "I think so. Who did we trip over?"

Frank was already examining the body. "The guard," he said. "Apparently the thief knocked him out and left him on the steps."

"Is he hurt?"

"I don't know. His pulse is okay, but he's unconscious," Frank replied.

"Let's tell the guard at the main gate what happened," Joe suggested. "Then we'll see if we can find the thief's trail."

The Hardys ran to the entrance and talked to the man on duty, who had not seen the thief enter. He promised to look after the unconscious guard on the stairs, when Nancy pulled up in their car.

Turn to page 93.

"Hurry, get in," she called out. "I saw a suspect crawl over the wall of the Tower. He got into a black van and drove away. Maybe we can still follow him."

Frank jumped in the front beside Nancy and Joe climbed in the back. Nancy turned the car around quickly and then began to pursue the fugitive.

Turn to page 113.

94

As Frank and Joe walked into Bromley Hall with Robin, they were met by Nancy, Philip, Elizabeth, Mr. Drew, and Jenkins.

"You found the sword!" Nancy exclaimed in excitement. "I spent the entire time searching for it in the maze."

Philip pointed to Robin.

"That's the strange man I caught a glimpse of going into the maze," he said. "I tried to follow him, but he got away."

Jenkins walked up to the old man, who now looked ashamed of himself.

"Were you behind all this, Thomas?" the butler asked. Then he explained to the visitors. "Thomas likes to think he is Robin Hood and the Bromley estate is Sherwood Forest."

"Someone has to keep up the tradition of England," the man in green muttered.

As Jenkins led Thomas off to the kitchen for a warm meal, he warned him, "We're going to call the Sheriff of Nottingham one of these days!"

Frank and Joe chuckled as they watched Robin go. Then Frank asked Nancy, "What about the statue?"

"No one pushed it," the sleuth explained. "A maid knocked it over accidentally and was afraid to confess at first. Now let's open this sword!"

Carson Drew pressed the sapphire eye of the lion carved into the hilt and twisted it to the right. The hilt separated from the blade.

Turn to page 95.

A document was hidden inside. Mr. Drew pulled it out and studied it for several minutes.

"It's a land deed!" he finally announced. "And here's a note with it."

Everyone waited in hushed anticipation as the lawyer read the message.

"Many years ago," he said, "Lord Bromley purchased a large piece of land in America, at my father's suggestion. In his letter, he asked that I sell the land, which is now worth millions of dollars. He wants the profits to be used to create a large public park on part of his estate here in England."

"Wait till Robin Hood hears about this!" Joe laughed. "Lord Bromley is giving him Sherwood Forest!"

END

96

Frank and Joe ran toward Philippe Arnolde as he neared his red Triumph. The young man looked over his shoulder as he heard the Hardys approaching him. Then he quickly leaped into his sports car and put the key in the ignition. But before he could start the engine, Joe jumped in beside him and grabbed the keys.

"Good work," Frank said to his brother, as he came around to the other side of Philippe.

Just then, a burly, bearded man pounced on Frank from behind! Philippe took advantage of Joe's surprise at the sudden attack and grabbed back his keys. With the same motion, he landed a punch squarely on Joe's jaw.

The young detective recovered quickly and managed to drag the Frenchman out of the car and onto the driveway. After a short struggle, he had the impostor pinned to the ground. At the same moment, Frank overpowered the burly man with a judo throw, aiming his assailant's body against the side of the sports car. The huge man collapsed unconscious on the ground.

"So, you're the snake who stole Lord Bromley's sword," Joe accused Philippe. He searched the man's pockets and found several papers. After examining them, the young detective deduced that they had been stolen from Bromley Hall.

Turn to page 97.

"My plan would have worked," Philippe snarled, "if you hadn't interfered."

Nancy joined the Hardy boys after breaking the bad news to Elizabeth. She gave the impostor a look of disgust. Then her eyes fell upon the burly man sprawled on the ground.

"He's the one who locked me inside the hut!" she exclaimed.

"If he had followed my orders," Philippe said meanly, "you never would have gotten out."

Nancy turned away from Arnolde and said to Frank and Joe, "Once the police take them away, Bromley Hall will be rid of its curse. By the way, I found out the truth about the statue. A maid who was dusting upstairs knocked it over accidentally. She was afraid to admit it at first, but finally confessed to Elizabeth."

"Let's call the police now," Frank said with satisfaction. "The case of the Silver Knight's sword is closed."

END

98

Carson Drew was waiting as Nancy entered Bromley Hall, carrying the knight's sword.

"You found it!" he said proudly, hugging his daughter. "We just learned how the statue fell. A maid toppled it while dusting."

Just then, a teary-eyed Elizabeth came into the hallway from the drawing room. She squared her shoulders and made a brave announcement. "I just caught Philip going through my grandfather's desk. He had removed valuable papers and was about to steal them. When I questioned him, he ran off without answering me."

"Elizabeth, your grandfather wanted to tell you something before he died," Nancy explained. "It's all here in this letter he had hidden in the knight's sword."

Elizabeth took the paper and went into the drawing room to read it alone. Nancy turned to her father and explained to him what it said. "It was Philip who stole the sword. He is an impostor and a criminal. Frank and Joe went after him."

Then she reached up and placed the sword back where it belonged in the hand of the Silver Knight. "One thing's for certain," she said, "the Silver Knight saved Elizabeth from the curse of marrying Philippe Arnolde!"

END

The two criminals shoved Joe ahead of them, out a door at the rear of the cellar, and into a dark alley.

"Don't make a sound," the older man hissed at him, "or you'll regret it."

Joe stumbled through the alley with his captors, trying to form a plan of escape. Soon, he heard the soft lapping of water against a dock. A minute later, he saw the Thames River.

"Get into the boat," Lopez ordered Ramón. "I'll stash the loot in the hold." He scrambled on board and disappeared downstairs.

Joe eyed Ramón as the young man roughly forced him onto the boat.

"He'll get a fortune for that necklace, you know," Joe whispered.

Ramón angrily stared toward the hold.

"He's making you do all the dirty work," Joe continued, "while he rakes in the money."

"You be quiet!" Ramón rasped.

Turn to page 100.

100

Joe anxiously waited for Lopez to come back up on deck. Finally, the man appeared at the top of the stairs, with a satisfied grin on his face.

"Where did you put the necklace?" Ramón demanded.

"It's none of your business," the criminal snarled. "Now get off the boat. Your work is done."

A look of wild anger flashed in Ramón's eyes. He lunged for Lopez and pushed him toward the side of the boat. The swarthy man staggered and swung out at his attacker. While they were battling fiercely with each other, Joe quickly moved to a spot nearby where he had seen a fishing knife stuck in the wood. He rubbed the ropes around his wrists against its sharp blade until he was freed. At that moment, Ramón landed a punch that sent Lopez flying overboard. Joe quickly rushed to Ramón's side and, after a brief struggle, overpowered the young man. Then he tied him to the wheel of the boat.

Lopez, meanwhile, was frantically splashing around in the water. A bobby's shrill whistle pierced the air as Joe was about to go after him.

Turn to page 101.

"What's going on here?" the policeman asked as he came aboard the boat.

"There's a thief in the water," Joe said, and pointed to the criminal flailing about in the waves.

While the bobby dragged the man from the river, Joe went into the hold to recover the knight's sword and the diamond necklace. As he brought the treasures back on deck, they both sparkled in the moonlight.

"Well!" the bobby exclaimed in surprise. "What have you got there?"

"The loot," Joe said and reported what had happened.

"You really caught a couple of big-time crooks!" the policeman said. "Good show! Would you like to join the London police force? We need detectives like you."

Joe laughed. "No, thanks. I'd like to resume my vacation!"

END

102

As Nancy twisted off the hilt of the knight's sword, an old silver key fell out and clattered to the cellar floor.

Joe bent down and examined the small, intricate key. "What does it unlock?" he asked.

"Perhaps this holds the secret," Nancy said, pulling a note out of the hilt.

She opened the folded paper and read the mysterious message. " 'This key locked away my broken heart. It will open a treasure for my granddaughter Elizabeth. Look under the rose.' The rose . . ." Nancy repeated curiously, looking at Elizabeth. "What did Lord Bromley mean by that?"

"I don't know," Elizabeth answered, baffled.

Just then, they heard Carson Drew's worried voice call down into the cellar. "Nancy?"

"We'll be right up, Dad," Nancy called back. She turned to Frank and Joe. "Let's start searching for the rose right away."

Turn to page 110.

"There's the river called the Serpentine," Frank shouted to Joe as they hurried through the empty park. "But where could Nancy be?"

As the brothers came to a bridge that crossed the Serpentine, they saw a lone rowboat anchored in the middle of the river.

Joe stopped and stared. "There's a body in that boat!" he declared. "I'll go and investigate."

He quickly pulled off his jacket, shirt, and shoes, then jumped into the water. With strong strokes, he swam to the boat.

Turn to page 105.

"It's Nancy!" he shouted a moment later. "She's alive!" He climbed into the boat and rowed it to the bank where Frank hurried to meet him.

Nancy had regained consciousness when the Hardy boys lifted her out onto the ground.

"The sword," she said drowsily, pointing to the silver weapon in the boat. "They gave me the sword."

"Let's get you back to the hotel," Frank said with concern. "We'll look at the sword later."

Turn to page 106.

106

Back in her hotel room, Nancy told the Hardys the story of her capture. After being pulled into the car, she had been drugged. Her next memory was of Joe getting into the boat with her on the Serpentine.

Frank picked up the sword of the Silver Knight. "I suspect that whatever Lord Bromley hid in here is gone since the crooks gave up the sword." He twisted off the hilt and examined it.

"I was right," the young sleuth said with disappointment. "It's empty."

At that moment, Fenton Hardy came into the room, looking for Frank and Joe. The young detectives explained everything that had happened that day to him. When they were finished, the investigator spoke to them in a serious voice.

"Lord Bromley was a secret agent for the British government. Before his death, he was assigned to the same case that I'm presently working on. You have become involved in a dangerous, international spy ring. I'll have to go to Miss Berenski's house immediately."

"May we come along, Dad?" Frank pleaded.

"Yes, all right," Fenton Hardy replied. Then he looked at Nancy. "You need some rest, though, young lady."

"I guess you're right," Nancy admitted wearily.

"Talk to you later," Joe said as they left.

Turn to page 117.

"So, you thought you were being clever, sneaking into my castle," the old man said. "My servant, Ivan, told me you had followed him here from the Tower."

The three sleuths shuddered as the huge man who had stolen the weapons stepped into the glow of the lantern. He held a wicked-looking knife in his hand.

"Where shall I take them, Count Christo?" he asked with a nasty leer.

"Let them see my collection of arms, so they know how powerful we are. Then take them to the prisoner's tower," Count Christo said.

Prodded by Ivan, Nancy, Frank, and Joe followed Count Christo into the castle. They were led into a magnificent room decorated with antique weapons and suits of armor. Many swords hung on the walls.

"Soon, I will own all the great weapons in the realm," Count Christo raved madly. Then he turned threateningly to the young detectives. "And don't think that you will be able to stop me. Ivan, take them away."

Ivan motioned the trio from the room and then ordered them up a staircase of twisting, narrow steps. He followed behind with the long knife in his hand. At the top, he shoved them into a cell-like room.

Turn to page 108.

108

"You'll stay here," he commanded, "until the count decides what to do with you."

Nancy, Frank, and Joe looked at each other anxiously as he slammed the door shut.

After Ivan had gone, Frank went to the narrow window of their cell. "It's a long drop into the moat," he said. "But there's a drainpipe I can reach from here. I could try to climb down, swim across the moat, and go for help."

"I hope that crazy count doesn't keep anything dangerous in the water, like sharks," Nancy cautioned. "It's a risky plan, Frank."

"And the drainpipe may break off," Joe added.

"But it is our only hope for escape," Frank said urgently, getting up on the windowsill. "And the drainpipe looks sturdy enough."

"Perhaps," Nancy said as she reached into her shoulder bag. "But I have another idea."

If you want to hear Nancy's plan for escape, turn to page 109.

If you think Frank should climb down the castle wall and go for help, turn to page 120.

Nancy pulled her camera from her shoulder bag. Carefully, she detached the electronic flash from the camera body.

"Watch," she said to Frank and Joe. Then she fired the electronic flash out the window of their cell. Its brilliant light pierced the night sky. "I have enough batteries to keep using this flash for several hours," she explained. "Someone is sure to see it and become suspicious."

Nancy sat down beside the window and aimed her unusual SOS signal into the night.

Turn to page 121.

110

The young detectives and Elizabeth went upstairs, and everyone gathered in the drawing room. Nancy showed her father the key and Lord Bromley's note, while Elizabeth told him how Jenkins had betrayed the family's trust.

"So that explains why he ran from the house in such a panic," Mr. Drew said. "By the way, Elizabeth, one of your young maids came crying to me a few minutes ago. She confessed that she toppled the statue at the top of the stairs while she was dusting."

Frank had been staring out a window, deep in thought. Suddenly, he turned to face everyone with an excited look in his eyes. "Before we came into the house, I saw a round, stained-glass window on the second floor. The glass formed the shape of a rose."

"The rose window, of course!" Elizabeth exclaimed. "It's in a little room that was my grandmother's before she died."

"Good thinking, brother," Joe said, heading for the door.

"Wait a minute," Elizabeth said thoughtfully. "I just remembered another rose. It's a real one that is planted near my grandmother's grave. Grandfather always took special care of it."

"Let's go see it right now," Nancy urged.

If you want to go with Frank and Joe, turn to page 111.

If you want to follow Nancy and Elizabeth, turn to page 114.

Frank and Joe entered the small room with the rose window. The sun filtered through the stained glass in beautiful colors. Beneath the window was a seat made of inlaid wood.

"Let's check there," Frank suggested.

He began to press on the different parts of the patterned wood, testing its strength. Finally, he found a section that gave way under his touch.

"Look, Joe," he said. "It's like a puzzle. This piece of oak popped up as a handle."

He tugged sharply on the wood, and to his surprise, a large block of the window seat swung out.

Joe stared in awe. "We've found it!" he exclaimed, and removed a beautiful silver box from its hiding place.

Frank took the key from his pocket and fit it into the lock. Joe whistled softly as his brother opened the box. Inside was a glittering array of jewels! Embroidered on the velvet lining of the lid was the name Emily Bromley.

At that moment, Elizabeth and Nancy came into the room. Frank and Joe proudly handed the box to Elizabeth.

"Your treasure, my lady," Frank said with a sweeping bow.

Turn to page 112.

112

Elizabeth's eyes shone as brightly as the jewels inside the silver box.

"They were my grandmother's," she explained. "No one ever knew what happened to them."

"No one except Lord Bromley," Nancy added with a smile, "and the Silver Knight."

END

"That's the van, two blocks ahead of us," Nancy said excitedly a few minutes later. "I recognize its taillights."

"I wish we had a transmitter with us," Frank said anxiously. "Then we could call the police."

"We'll just have to make sure we keep up with him," Nancy said, straining her eyes to watch the road ahead.

The streets of London were nearly deserted after midnight. She was able to trail the van through the East End of the city and out into the countryside.

"I wonder where he's going?" Joe asked curiously as they followed the van onto a dark, narrow road.

Half an hour later, the sleuths watched as the fugitive made a sharp right turn and disappeared down a tree-lined drive.

"I think we'd better go past the drive and park down the road," Nancy suggested. "We can follow the rest of the way on foot."

After they had left the car, Nancy, Frank, and Joe crept back through the darkness. They started down the desolate driveway that wound to an unknown end.

Turn back to page 73.

114

Nancy and Elizabeth walked out of Bromley Hall into a light, drizzling rain.

"It's not far to the graveyard," Elizabeth assured her companion. "We'll take this path to its end."

The girls hurried down the flagstones that wound through thick bushes and trees. Nancy shivered as the cool, damp air penetrated her thin sweater. Within a short time, they arrived at an iron gate that was decorated with a small replica of the Silver Knight.

"All of the Bromleys are buried here," Elizabeth said as she pushed open the gate. "My grandmother died many years ago, when she was only twenty-nine."

"Where is the rose you told me about?" Nancy asked, eager to examine it.

Elizabeth led the way through the graveyard dotted with ancient monuments and towering trees.

"It's right here—" she started to say, but her words were choked by a scream.

Turn to page 118.

"I did!" the thief screamed madly. "And I would have been able to handle these boys also, but fate turned against me!" He continued to rave about his strength and the many weapons he had stolen.

"I think he's a little crazy," Frank whispered to the officer.

"We'll find out soon," the policeman replied. "He'll be questioned thoroughly at headquarters."

As the police and the Hardys were leading the prisoner outside, they were met by Nancy in front of the building.

"I found his car!" the girl said triumphantly. "He parked it in an alley around the corner."

One of the officers accompanied the young people to the criminal's large sedan, and the policeman opened its trunk. Inside was a stash of stolen weapons, including a long, graceful sword.

"It has a lion carved on its hilt. That must belong to the Silver Knight!" Frank exclaimed.

The policeman nodded. "Apparently, the thief hasn't bothered to unload the goods from previous capers," he said.

Half an hour later, the young detectives sat in Timothy Morgan's office and opened Lord Bromley's sword. Nancy's face lit up when she read the note inside.

"On this paper," she told Frank and Joe, "is the number to a secret safety deposit box. It contains enough money to pay the debts of the Bromley family."

Turn to page 116.

116

The three sleuths stood up to leave and said good-bye to Mr. Morgan.

"We'll come back to the Tower sometime—just as tourists," Frank told the curator.

Joe looked at his brother doubtfully. "I don't know about that, Frank. I never want to see the executioner's axe again . . . that's for sure!"

END

An hour later, Fenton Hardy had 40 Palace Gate surrounded by British security agents. Frank and Joe watched as their father knocked on the front door of the house. Miss Berenski opened it cautiously. Then everything started to happen all at once.

The young woman tried to run away into the street but was caught by a man guarding the front. Other agents entered the house from the rear and cornered two men trying to escape. Joe and Frank noticed a third spy climbing out onto the roof. They recognized him as the driver of the green car. Quickly they alerted a security official, who stopped the man's getaway.

After the agents had taken away their prisoners, Fenton Hardy turned to his sons. "These people were spies working within the British government. I was informed today that a top-level official in the foreign office suddenly disappeared. We suspect that he was a double agent. And I believe that he was tipped off after Miss Berenski and her cohorts found the message in the knight's sword."

"You mean that Lord Bromley's secret was the name of a British government official who was really a double agent?" Joe asked excitedly.

"That's right," Mr. Hardy said. "I'm sure we'll catch him once these people talk. I'm going down to the secret service right now to wind up the case. I have a long night's work ahead of me."

"And we'll visit Elizabeth in the morning," Frank said. "She'll be delighted to get the sword back!"

END

118

A man with a shovel whirled around at the sound of the young woman's voice. Nancy observed that he had dug up a rose bush near the grave of Elizabeth's grandmother.

"So," the man said with a snicker. "You figured it out, too, Miss Elizabeth."

"It's Charles, the family chauffeur," Elizabeth explained to Nancy. Then she asked the man, "How did you know about my grandfather's note?"

"Jenkins and I were partners, you see," he said with a mean laugh. "I was in the cellar the whole time you were opening the sword. I got there from upstairs by the hidden staircase."

"Did you push over that statue?" Nancy demanded.

"I didn't push it!" the chauffeur answered defensively. "I knocked it over by accident. All I want is the treasure. And now that Jenkins has run off, it's all mine."

"I wouldn't be too sure about that," Nancy said firmly.

"Oh, but here it is," Charles said, hitting a metal box with the end of his shovel. "Look under the rose, that's what Lord Bromley wrote. As soon as I figure out what to do with you two, I'll be living like a king."

The chauffeur began to walk toward Nancy and Elizabeth, holding the shovel tightly in his hands.

Turn to page 119.

Suddenly, the chauffeur was grabbed from behind by the strong arms of Joe and Frank Hardy!

"You got here just in time!" Nancy cried in relief, and the fear in Elizabeth's face changed to a look of triumph.

"Thanks for digging up the treasure for us," Joe said to Charles. "But you won't be living like a king where you're going!"

While the Hardys pulled the protesting man away to the house, Nancy reached down and removed an old box of darkened metal from under the rose bush. Then she took the silver key from her skirt pocket and handed it to Elizabeth. "Here," she said with a smile. "You open the treasure!"

With shaking hands, the young woman fit the key into the lock. As she lifted the lid, an expression of awe came over her face.

"My grandmother's jewels!" she exclaimed softly.

Nancy gazed at the beautiful gems in the box. Lord Bromley had buried them near his young, beloved wife. Now the secret of the knight's sword had brought them to his granddaughter.

END

120

Frank swung his body over the narrow windowsill and began his dangerous descent. He inched down the wall, trying to make as little noise as possible. Several times, the brackets holding the drainpipe creaked dangerously, but Frank made it to the bottom of the castle as Nancy and Joe watched worriedly from the window.

Finally, he dropped into the moat and, with strong strokes, swam to the other side.

After he had climbed onto the bank, he waved to his friends. Nancy and Joe returned the gesture, then Frank slipped away into the darkness.

Turn to page 122.

An hour later, Nancy, Frank, and Joe watched the police surround the castle. The drawbridge was lowered, and there were sounds of a struggle. Then Count Christo and Ivan were dragged outside.

Finally, the young people were freed.

"We saw your signal," the local police chief told them. "We have been watching this place for weeks, and wondered what was going on."

"Count Christo, as he calls himself, was stealing the finest weapons in England," Frank explained. "Our search for a sword that was taken from Bromley Hall put us on the thieves' trail."

The young detectives led the chief into the weapons room, where Nancy went over to the wall and examined the swords hanging there. At last, she found one with a lion carved on its hilt. The animal's eye was fashioned from a beautiful sapphire. She took down the sword, pressed the eye, and twisted the hilt to the right. Inside the handle, she found a folded piece of paper. Excitedly, she read its contents to the others.

" 'Bromley Hall will be saved by the Silver Knight. I instruct Elizabeth to sell the knight to one of the nation's museums. It is of great value, and the money from the sale will pay the family's debts. Lord Bromley.' "

"Hooray!" Joe exclaimed. "The secret of the Silver Knight has been discovered!"

"And a gang of thieves has been caught, thanks to your efforts," the police chief said. "Congratulations on an excellent job!"

END

122

Two hours later, Nancy and Joe heard loud voices in the castle below them. There were sounds of a struggle. Then Frank opened the door to the cell. He was holding a beautiful sword with a lion carved in its hilt.

"Boy, are we glad to see you!" Nancy and Joe cried out.

Frank grinned. "You didn't think I'd leave you here, did you?" He held up the sword. "I searched the weapons room and found this."

"Do you think it's the Silver Knight's?" Nancy was so excited that she jumped up and down.

"We'll soon find out," Frank replied, pressing on the lion's sapphire eye. He twisted the hilt to the right and pulled it off the sword. A small piece of paper was folded inside. Excitedly, he read its contents to Nancy and Joe.

" 'Bromley Hall will be saved by the Silver Knight. I instruct Elizabeth to sell it to one of the nation's museums. It is of great value, and the money from the sale will pay the debts of the family. Lord Bromley.' "

Nancy breathed a sigh of relief. "Elizabeth will be glad to hear that news." Then she added with a tired laugh, "Now I want to get out of this cell. I've lived in the Middle Ages long enough!"

END